CH00841044

BBC CHILDREN'S BOOKS
Published by the Penguin Group
Penguin Books Ltd, 80 Strand, London WC2R 0RL, England
Penguin Putnam Inc., 375 Hudson Street, New York, New York 10014, USA
Penguin Books Australia Ltd, 250 Camberwell Road, Camberwell, Victoria 3124, Australia
Canada, India, New Zealand, South Africa
First published in 2002 by BBC Worldwide Limited
This edition published by BBC Children's Books, 2005
10 9 8 7 6 5 4 3 2
Text by Sara Carroll
Illustrations by Magic Island
Text, design and illustrations © BBC Children's Books, 2005
The Tweenies name, logo and characters are trademarks of the
British Broadcasting Corporation and are used under licence. © BBC 1998-2001
Tweenies is produced by Tell-Tale Productions for BBC Television
BBC and logo © and ™ BBC 1996. CBeebies and logo ™ BBC. © BBC 2002
All rights reserved.
ISBN 1 405 90093 8
Printed in Italy

Make It Big!

Milo and Jake had a problem. They were building the castle of Sir Milo the Great, but there was a big hole in the wall.

"Could you pass me some bricks to put in here, please, Jake?" Milo asked.

Jake took one out of the box.

"No mate, I wanted one to fill this space," said Milo. "That one's too small."

Jake looked in the box.

"Sorry, Milo, but there aren't any big enough bricks to fill that space."

Milo sighed. How was he going to finish the castle?

On the other side of the room, Max had a problem, too. He, Fizz and Bella were taking some old pictures off the wall and there were large dark marks where the pictures had been.

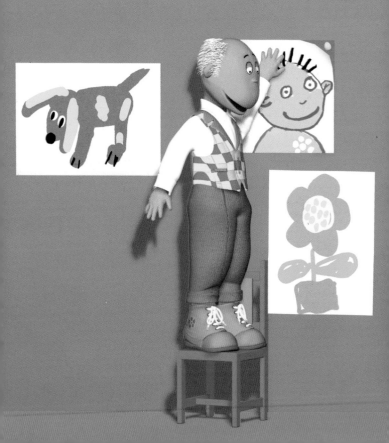

"We're going to need something pretty big to cover up these marks," said Max.

Jake came over to watch.

"How's the castle, Jake?" asked Bella.

"We've run out of big bricks," he explained. Then he looked up.

"Eeurgh! Look at those big marks on the wall. You'd better cover them up with something, Max!"

Judy was showing Milo how to finish the castle when Jake got back.

"Look, Jakey! The castle of Sir Milo the Great is now finished!" said Milo.

"Wow! How did you do that?" asked Jake in surprise.

"Judy showed me how three little bricks can fill the same space as one big one," Milo explained.

That reminded Jake and Milo of a song they knew. Bella and Fizz joined in.

There are hundreds of grains of sand
    on a beach,
Thousands of hairs on your head.
Can you count all the bricks in the
    walls of your house?
Or the bubbles in your bath before bed?

Take a look at the world around us,
At the things that we use and we see.
There are so many things made from
    smaller things.
Come and look at some more with me.

How many pieces make up an orange?
How many trees in a wood?
Can you count all the blades of grass
   in a field?
You'd find millions of them if you could.

Lots of petals make up a flower,
Hundreds of sticks make a nest.
How many crumbs in a piece of cake?
I like counting those up the best!

So, take a look at the world around us,
At the things that we use and we see.
There are so many things made from
        smaller things.
Spot some more and show them to me.

The Tweenies started to look around.

"A jigsaw puzzle is made of lots of small bits!" said Fizz.

"And lots of little beads make up this necklace," shouted Bella.

"And my huge lunch is made up of lots of big sandwiches!" laughed Milo.

"And castles are made with lots of bricks," added Jake.

"That's given me an idea," said Max.

Max called the Tweenies over to the messy table. There were piles of tiny squares of coloured paper.

Max put a big sheet of plain paper on the floor and started to explain.

"All that singing about big things made of little things made me think about my problem on the wall. I thought we could make a mosaic. That's a big picture made from lots of little bits stuck down."

"Stick-a-rooney!" shouted Milo.

The Tweenies rushed to get their overalls.

"All we need to do now is decide what the picture will be," said Max.

Milo wanted to do a castle, of course.

Jake liked the idea of the seaside.

Fizz wanted a fairy grotto and Bella wanted a house.

In the end, they agreed to make a picture that everyone would like.

"You can each have your own corner to decorate," Max promised.

Judy told the Tweenies where to put the different colours.

"That's right, Jake. You need lots of red and yellow bits," she said. She helped Bella, Milo and Fizz with their sticking, too.

Doodles tried to help them, but he got bits of paper stuck all over him, so Judy had to clean him up.

Doodles wasn't the only one getting in a mess. Soon there was paper everywhere!

Finally, the Tweenies put down their gluing brushes and stood up to have a look.

"It's fantastic!" gasped Bella.

"And it's huge!" said Milo.

The paper was filled from end to end.
Everyone had helped to make a really
special picture.

"Excellent!" said Max. "Now let's see what it looks like on the wall."

"Oh, we've made a great big Doodles," said Jake.

"And it fits over those big marks!" said Fizz.

"It looks great," said Judy. "Well done, everyone!"

Jake stared at the picture in amazement.

"Who would have thought that all those teeny tiny pieces of paper would make such a great big picture!" he gasped.

"And such a huge, sticky mess!"
said Judy.

THE END